THE VOICE OF THE SWORD

2.0

The Voice Of The Sword 2.0
Copyright © 2023 by Joseph L Sinkfield.

Published in the United States of America

Library of Congress Control Number: 2024901089
ISBN   Paperback: 979-8-89091-414-9
ISBN   Hardback: 979-8-89091-415-6
ISBN   eBook: 979-8-89091-416-3

All rights reserved. No part of this publication may be reproduced, stored in a retrieval system or transmitted in any way by any means, electronic, mechanical, photocopy, recording or otherwise without the prior permission of the author except as provided by USA copyright law.

The opinions expressed by the author are not necessarily those of ReadersMagnet, LLC.

ReadersMagnet, LLC
10620 Treena Street, Suite 230 | San Diego, California, 92131 USA
1.619. 354. 2643 | www.readersmagnet.com

Book design copyright © 2023 by ReadersMagnet, LLC. All rights reserved.

Cover design by Jhiee Oraiz
Interior design by Daniel Lopez

THE VOICE OF THE SWORD

2.0

Joseph L Sinkfield

ReadersMagnet, LLC

Thank you for your purchase of The Voice of the Sword book.

This has not been an easy journey, after sending my manuscript to Covenant books my manuscript was sent to Xulon Press for publication. This was not a rewarding experience or easy. The first time sent I was put on a payment plan to pay for their services, which was fine with me being that the cost was in the thousands. I put a thousand dollar down payment on my bill thinking that it would expedite the process. I would receive calls from their Publication Coordinator on a regular basis. This went on for several months until a certain level of payment was obtained, then I stopped hearing from them, also my calls would go unanswered. I called to voice my concerns, this is when I was told that the coordinator working on my project was moved to another part of their company, while payments continued to be removed from my account. Feeling ghosted, not hearing from this guy, I put a stop payment on my account. This got an immediate response from them. I also changed my card number for them not to have my information, I decided to send the company money orders to complete my balance. Fully paid and looking forward to being published, as usual I was being ghosted, the company apologized profusely and never produced a finished product claiming to be a Christian organization and would work diligently through to the end. After the span of several months, not hearing from them, someone else in the company called to inform me that they could not complete the project and that they would be sending me a refund minus publishing services performed on my manuscript, the only thing that was tangible of them giving me was an author's kit which included a how to book a marker and a package of instant coffee.

This process went on for approximately sixteen months with the ten-dollar author kit. I was incredibly upset. Not wanting to give up on my project, feeling that the people of God needed encouragement, and direction to the truth. Several months went by of me being upset, knowing that the book would be a great benefit to the readers. I decided to put my feelings aside and not give up. I decided to send the manuscript thru the same company a second time thinking that maybe God was working on my humility, patience and pride. The same coordinator that worked on my book the first time was now assigned to me the second time, familiar with all the problems and situations that I experienced the first time. Fool me once, shame on you. Fool me twice shame on me. I was referred to a coordinator of her choice and that person would stay on the course and produce a finished product. For the payment, I decided to only pay the down payment and not tie my finances up for two years hoping to publish a book. Again, she apologized adamantly about how I was treated the last time, so I waited and waited. After approximately seven months, another member of their staff called me to say that they could not publish my book because it had a lot of objectionable material in it and that they would be sending my down payment back to me. Part of my background is in teaching; I have taught in a formal church and reached the position of assistant pastor. I volunteered in the prison system to teach the inmates the Bible. I was a classroom and behind the wheel instructor for MVA and a private school instructor for over twenty years. Through those years, I have learned that students may read but don't read with understanding or comprehend what they read. I have over the years devised a plan to start them on the road of comprehension and that is the who, what, when, where, why and how method of study. Apply these principles to all reading sessions and you're well on your way to comprehend what you have read. Students learn in many ways, mainly these, repetition, sight and sounding out a sentence. In my book there are no pictures available and repetition as a tool is not practical.

Before each chapter or discussion, I will give a scripture as a subtext for them to study. Using this process, the study of the subtext will point the reader in the proper direction to make sure that they have the writer's interpretation. Keeping your carnal mind under subjective state, accepting an interpretation because of what you were taught or has been accepted as a way of worship removing of your opinion, conclusions and accusations we make against God. That takes careful intense study, the Christian's Ephesians war clothes protects the mind, the helmet of salvation. The Bible is written in a mystery, conclusions are not easily obtained, an opportunity to enter the writers thought process. Then as the writer I will begin to dissect and explain what you are reading. I may pose a question to give the reader a direction to follow, looking at the Bible's example to see if it lines up with other books and thinking along the same lines, understandable.

The Voice of The Sword left off with the scripture in Luke 24:13-53. Jesus on the road to Emmaus, found several of the Apostles coming from the sepulcher expecting Jesus to be from another town, he began to expound and breakdown the scriptures to them, starting at Moses, he began to explain the scriptures about himself. That was not the important part. It was that they did not recognize Jesus even though many of the followers who were with him started to follow him during John's baptism. Jesus always took these followers aside and explained all his teachings after every sermon and they still don't recognize him. Luke 24:31.

What of his second coming? The world has the KJV Bible, Google and all manner of people making claims but until Jesus opens you're understanding, you won't see him, won't find him or hear him. When you find him, you make statements, testify and announce to the world, God is in you. 1 John 4:1-11.

The world is experiencing war's pestilence, violence and the beast nature is growing and making itself known. Christians should be confessing, testifying God's presence and love should abides in them. Either they are speaking the truth about the divine nature of God or speaking a lie. Careful study of the scriptures will give an accurate description of God's nature, don't limit your study on his nature but apply your study to other things, people and scripture. The conclusion you obtain must be consistent and in-line with other scriptures to make sure that you don't use your natural mind and disparage anyone or speak of them in an opinionated way.

In the beginning, God created man after His image, after His likeness. He blessed the male and female that He created, and told them to be fruitful and multiply. Then Genesis 2:5 says that there was not a man to till the ground and He formed a man from the dust of the ground and called his name Adam. This needs to be explained and lined up with the other scriptures. God is a spirit, therefore man was made after the image of God, a spirit so there was a man in the physical form who will till the ground, a man who was formed from the dust of the ground and was called Adam. Now the two parts of Adam were spiritual and flesh. The spiritual part is a spirit that is an eternal being and if God lived then man would live after the spirit that is an eternal being. After the death of the flesh, the other part would go back to the ground where the Lord God formed him. Hebrews 9:27. 2 Corinthians 4:18.

The problem is with us is we don't look at the scripture with the spiritual understanding, we look at it with our opinion or with our carnal, free will. We rationalize our interpretations, conclusions and understanding when we are making judgements and apply them to God, accusing Him of being totally opposite of His nature. I want to pose a challenge at this point. Write down on a piece of paper the nature of God, and the attributes of what you believe God to be. Place it aside and do the same for Adam, the serpent Cain and Abel. You can save these papers as a reference guide for further study. John 3:6.

Don't arrive so quickly at your conclusion, your conclusion may take years. When it comes to an interpretation, be able to distinguish between a spiritual understanding and your carnal, human will or opinion. Be honest first with God, then to yourself to be able to admit where you are wrong. I suggest you to study a scripture, Genesis 3:1, then I also suggest that you study the two verses in the bible. Rightly dividing and a clear understanding could mean salvation to the reader. Follow closely. This is the first time that the serpent was mentioned. Do not draw a conclusion way too early. The bible is written in a mystery. God would not place something in there without a purpose or meaning. This format should pique your interest to go deeper than just reading, and missing very important clues. James 1:5.

Sometimes there is nothing written which would pique your interest or form questions about the topic. The first thing to establish is that Moses wrote the bible inspired by God, its foundation is true and if you don't understand it, ponder on the statement and move on. Since it is written, I must believe it just like he said, he was a serpent and a beast different than any other beast. He said to the woman something that God said. He was a serpent, quoted God and spoke also who he was, a male and a beast. Consider his interpretation, he began quoting God. This statement implies him knowing God or spending time with God before being in the garden, he communicated with the woman meaning he was intelligent, by what he is saying we can see that he had ulterior motives, then he lied by adding one word to God's statement, and appealed to the woman's free will, carnal mind and opinion. The tree of knowledge of good and evil was literally a fruit tree, Eve formed the conclusion that it was good for food, and pleasant to the eyes. Instead of a spiritual understanding, it was the lust of the eyes and the lust of the flesh that she allowed to win. The scriptures say that the eyes of both were opened and they realized that they were naked. Once they both ate of the tree, they died spiritually not physically, they began to exhibit not God nature but human nature. If ever there was a time that the beast could get at the woman, it's at that moment, his motives are becoming clear, maybe this was not the only time he talked alone with the woman to impart his wisdom with other things taken place. The voice of the Lord God is always with us the entire day. Very important, Adam believed the lie told to him by the serpent and Eve. They were ashamed, naked and hid themselves from God. Adam and Eve made clothes to cover up their nakedness, pointed an accusing finger until they got down to the serpent, the beast. The first thing God did to the beast, the serpent was to curse him, the first curse, then to place enmity between the serpent and the woman and the serpent's seed and the woman's seed. Eating a piece of the fruit will not destroy a person's spiritual life or cause them to die, it will give knowledge or understanding that you are naked and make you ashamed of your body. The Lord God cursed the serpent down to his belly to eat the dust of the ground all the days of his life. Consider this, God speaking, would God know whether something other than eating fruit took place in the garden? He started the process with a curse, placing enmity between the serpent and the woman, and didn't stop there. He continued to the serpent's children. With God making this statement, He knows something for him to start punishment between the serpent and the woman, and the serpent's seed and the woman's seed. Making that statement, the serpent had to have a seed and the woman had to have a seed because God said it, just like it was said, "Let there be light" and there was light, the scripture must be fulfilled for it has to come to pass. Ecclesiastes 3:17-21 KJV.

An attribute of God is all knowing. There is a reason these statements are made that the serpent had to have children. Romans 8:7-9. For the woman, God said I will greatly multiply your pain during thy conception. Following the same line of reasoning, the children will cause pain during conception which is an effect with activities with the serpent or beast. The last part of that statement, God gave Eve back to Adam and he would rule over her. Desire was mentioned earlier, it was established that she was his wife, now she is given back to Adam. All the statements from the curse to statements spoken by God refers to carnal activities knowledge that would cause someone to be ashamed. Genesis 4:1.

Through studying all the things that was spoken to the beast, his seed was curse the enmity, God following the same direction, conception focusing on His knowing all the things that took place in the garden between the serpent and the woman punished them accordingly like a punishment fit for the crime. The punishment is not consistent with eating fruit. The serpent deceived the woman to believe him instead of believing God's statement of surely dying. Through her carnal mind, lust of the eyes and accepting the serpent's interpretation of what God said, implies other meetings between the serpent and the woman. Romans 3:4.

The carnal mind that cannot understand spiritual things would have you disparage God as the writers' preachers, question the validity of the bible, and accuse them of slanderous lies, all in the attempt to prove that you are correct in your opinion. Repent, drop your carnal way of thinking. Always be on the side with God. On the woman's part, what she did was to consider what was said to her, used her free will, the lust of the eyes and carnal mind to believe the message of the serpent. The devil may have taken notice that she was still alive and did not die, but she died spiritually, separated from God's spirit. She needed to realize that was the most important thing. If you know anything about God, you should understand that this all-knowing merciful God make provisions for the fall. Just because Eve fell did not make her any less the child of God through her actions. When Adam awoke from his sleep he called Eve his wife, he was operating with the spiritual mind. The same mind God allowed him to name all the animals, now that he died spiritually and no longer have that mind, no longer have that authority, now operates in the carnal realm. His punishment was because he listened to his wife, those statements were very specific, and because he fell, it did not make him any less God's son, creation of or in God's image. God's focus was not on the fruit or the tree of knowledge of good and evil, it was on listening to the voice of his wife and them both operating in their free will, carnal mind and belief of the serpent's interpretation of God's word.

Adam's punishment fit the crime. Consider what you know about the tree of knowledge of good and evil. The serpent used it to convince Eve to disobey the Lord. It appealed to her human nature because it was pleasant to the eyes and as the word said, it is desirable to make one wise and good for food. All of that was written, she had to accept it and believe it. When she believed it, she did not believe God, she did not operate using a spiritual mind or understanding and opened it for all manner of evil. You can add any kind of foolish statement. Romans 8:1-39.

Eve no longer operating with a spiritual mind began to operate in her natural mind considering that that wisdom was appealing to her emotions. The word desire is mentioned again by God in her punishment. It has been established that she was his wife for Adam and now God is specifying that there was a change in her desire and God gave her back to Adam. An investigation needs to be done on the word desire and who it was directed toward. The only other male figure in the garden was the serpent, the beast. Genesis 3:16.

Food for thought, while operating in the carnal mind, what were the attributes of the serpent? Careful study will tell you that he was an angel that was clothed with every precious stone. He was a musician, convinced a third part of the angels to believe he would exalt his throne above the throne of God, was cast out of heaven into outer darkness. When God said let there be light and there was light, He showed up in the first book of Moses. He could not enter God's blessed creation, so he counterfeited a body to communicate with Eve not on a spiritual level but a physical level. Genesis 1:1.

Your carnal mind would visualize a red man in a red suit with horn pitchfork, a snake with feet and legs but, he was a beautiful being and pleasing to Eve's eyes. What about the spirit of God moving upon the face of the deep and waters? Genesis 1:2.

The book of Revelation 17:15 tells us what the waters represent, people, multitudes, nations and tongues. These were in the beginning before the first day. God made provisions for the serpent to counterfeit his creation, to have children by adding a seed in a body with a spirit that is totally opposite from God's. He can kill it, curse it, disrespect it, and not use the spiritual creation and put it in a devil's body. It is very simple to see how the serpent extended his campaign, not only to the third part of the heavenly body but people, nations' tongues. What are their attributes? They lie, they kill, they steal, and they hate God. On the outward, the scriptures say that the daughters of men were fair, they looked good to the sons of God. Genesis 6:1-2.

These sons of men operated with the carnal mind; they had a beast nature like their father. Because they were so like the sons of God in appearance, a mark was placed on them. Ecclesiastes 3:14-22. 1 John 3:7-15.

Your carnal mind wants to find fault with the bible. Speaking lies against it, saying it contradict itself. Anything to divert your mind from the truth. You must study the word. Make sure you have the writer's meaning, either implied or otherwise. Before you accuse someone, make sure you have all the facts. When you say that Adam was the father of Cain, the attributes came from Adam. Well God is accused of having an evil side and that sin entered the world by him. This is not a good thing to do, trying to apply an evil nature to God, it is not consistent. Study a lot, do longer search, and look deeper into the mysteries of God, hopefully you will begin to understand the divine nature of God. He will open you're understanding and point you in the proper direction. Challenge your mind and make sure you are looking at it with the proper focus. Isaiah 28:9-13. Psalms 34:8. 1. Peter 2:2-3.

The tree of life, as per observations of the scriptures, doesn't have many corresponding texts about it. It was important enough to write about it and nothing much said. Do you suppose this should pique your curiosity? What's so special about this tree? Why didn't the serpent use that tree to deceive the woman? Is it a fruit tree? Is it a bread tree? Or is it a word tree? What kind of fruit does a bread tree produce? John 6:63. 1 Corinthians 2:7-16. 2 Corinthians 4:18. John 6:26-65.

There are no interpretations about that tree, just that there is a flaming sword turning in all directions to protect the way of the tree of life. Genesis 3:22. Isaiah 35:8-9.

Eating a fruit from this tree will give you everlasting life, the sword is to remove carnal thoughts, the flesh and any beast. It implies a spiritual tree, a spiritual food and an important to man's spiritual life. Christian's adopt customs and ways of worship like every third Sunday, taking the communion when the devil counterfeited this. You say where two or three are gathered there is Jesus in the midst, it is specific you must eat his spiritual body and drink his blood so you will have life in you. Why are you symbolically playing church which is vain in its practice? Genesis 4:1.

When you partake of the unleavened bread and the wine, you confess that it is his body and his blood not discerning his body. By putting them before him in his presence, it is either you are speaking a lie or saying that God told you to continue this custom. You can't have it both ways. The Christian churches adopt this custom, why not the custom of sprinkling blood on the altar? Killing animals or putting blood on the doorposts and lentils.

Many of the customs of the people, if not all of them, when Christ came on the scene, why not this one also? It's easy to counterfeit and gullible followers, they easily believe it's the right thing to do. Psalms 34:8. Either you taste him, or you are playing church and will be under bondage, not discerning the Lord's body, eating and drinking that is harmful to their souls. Genesis 4:1.

Studying this scripture, it says Adam knew his wife Eve, and she conceived and bare Cain. Eve was saying that I've gotten a man from the Lord. Be reasonable, God in chapter 3:16, said I will multiply your pain during conception. Conception can only be derived from carnal knowledge, but this conception was between the serpent and the woman. Are you saying that God don't know what he was talking about? She would have to be already with child in chapter 3. Now her desire will be towards her husband, and he shall rule over her. The word implies her desire was focused on the serpent, the beast and she conceived. The punishment that was handed out then was also between the serpent's seed and the woman's seed which refers to children. Genesis 3:15. Because the scripture specifically said that enmity would be between the woman's seed and the serpent's seed, God said it. That was before Adam knew his wife Eve in chapter 4. Now that Adam understood that he was naked, who gave him the knowledge of producing a seed, a child, a baby? He got it from his wife. Where did she get this knowledge? From the serpent. If Eve was already with child, Adam could go through the motions one hundred times but it won't change the outcome of the serpent being there first. Don't jump to conclusions and assume Cain is the son of Adam.

What are God's attributes? Adams attributes, the serpent's and Cain's attributes? Call them attributes, nature, or characterizations. Study them before you draw your conclusions. Assign them to the right individual to continue with your study. Consider God's divine nature and Adam's nature would be the same, man and

Adam would be the same. Be consistent with your research, apply the same intensity or depth of study on every topic before you come to a conclusion. Decide where the focus should be following the writer's interpretation then you line up with it. Remember God blessed Adam and cursed the serpent and beast. The first child born was Cain, consider all the things said about him. Eve has gotten a man from the Lord. If he is from the Lord, who is she trying to convince? Examine the statement, she was the mother of all living, God created people, blessed people but who was Cain's father? Apply your study of nature and attribute it to the reference pages. Again, Eve conceived Cain and Abel, the two brothers. The scriptures pointed out the different characteristics of them in verse 4:2. Genesis 4:5. Romans 2:11.

Clearly, the bible says God did not have respect for Cain or his offering, that is a fact.

The only thing written about the two boys are they were born and prepared an offering for God. Genesis 4:11.

After the murder and lie, God cursed him just like how he cursed his father. Genesis 3:14. What about the enmity between the two sons? It shows up in the dispute between Abel and Cain. Which son is the serpent's seed and the woman's seed? Romans 2:11.

Apply the study guide you wrote and consider the attributes of Adam and the beast. Ask yourself, why would God have respect for one son and none for the other, if Adam fathered them both. An all-knowing God would know both their natures and have respect for whoever he chooses. Also, he would not take the spirit of his blessed creation and change it to a cursed body. If Adam had a son, he would have his attributes the same as God, because he would be born into the family. Cain also was born into a family, a bloodline of a family tree that will get no respect from God. 1 John 3:7-12. It was not in his nature to do good, and God knew and even gave him an opportunity to be accepted before the murder and lie. The circumcision practice for the people of God was to make a difference between the children of God and the children of the devil, the beast, the serpent. Genesis 3:14-15.

Either sons of God or the sons of men, their look where similar only God would know. Other than cursing the serpent, Cain and Canaan, they look the same outwardly but their soul, their nature are of beasts. The generations of Cain were fruitful and multiplied, sons and daughters were born unto them, known in that day the daughters of men. Genesis 6:1-7. Genesis 11:1-9. It was the mixing of the bloodlines that angered the Lord, the reason for the flood. Remember both were destroyed by the water, the only living was the family on the ark. 2 Timothy 2:15-26.

The word of God has been with man for over two thousand years. In that amount of time, man has been waiting for someone to break the bread of life, to explain spiritual things to them. Luke 16:20-31. To the saving of their souls. You have the beast nature, human nature and all kinds of evil prevailing in our time where evil symbolic customs, practices and ways of worship fill the churches. The government passing laws making it illegal to oppose them, people don't know which way to turn.

The Voice of The Sword (TVOTS) and TVOTS 2.0 is my opportunity to rightly divide the scriptures, to get specific, to have the reader read with understanding, based on bible facts not on a private interpretation. I did not just come by this knowledge yesterday. It's been accumulating over the past thirty or more years. This process should be applied to every study, every custom and every church tradition. I believe that God is giving me an opportunity to send this message across the country before changes are made that will be more difficult to follow. These last days, everybody is saying something. 1 Corinthians 14:10 1 Peter 4:17-19.

The point is not only to believe but how you believe. What you apply to that knowledge and how you follow with what conclusions you make. The two generations of people are finding their place in this mystery, testifying to what they believe, acting on that belief. You will stand alone before God and explain to him the road you traveled. There will be no exceptions, we pass through side windows and back doors that lead to right ways. Jesus is the way. You have that responsibility; find God and he will direct your path. Genesis 5:1-6.

This scripture gives the generations of Adam, blessed people, with God's attributes and likeness. In order to be part of Adam's generation one had to be born into it. Abel was not of the age of bearing children before Cain killed him. Cain was born first and then Abel from Eve who is the mother of all living, but who was his father? Study that fact. The first to be cursed by God was the serpent and the second was Cain in which God had no respect for him. Genesis 3:14. The only other male figure in the beginning was the serpent where God placed enmity between the woman's seed and the serpent's seed, the serpent's seed Cain. If the serpent was there first, the first seed would be his and not Adams. God said that there would be strife between the seeds, 3:15 and Cain murdered Abel, not attributes of Adam or

God. Cain's existence in the beginning with his people, in his towns and cities, Genesis 4:17-25.

None of these people were mentioned in Adams bloodline, his genealogy of generations began with Seth. Now I was very specific as a spiritual advisor pointing out the scriptures and where you should focus your attention, what things you should question considering the writer's clues on what is taking place. When doing so, you can make assumptions, misunderstandings and not believe the writers' account of the scriptures. You need to focus on what the writer implies and what is not written. Very important is how you believe what conclusions you accept and acting on them whether your interpretation is fact based or based on your nature, carnal mind. Romans 8:4-9.

Some of the points that we focused on are because of content and would not be published due to content, TVOTS is just the beginning that will help us see and understand spiritually the mysteries that have been their hundreds of years. TVOTS 2.0 was sent to the publishers several times, me having to make corrections. At the beginning of 2.0, I had to re-write it to satisfy the publishers. My manuscript was double spaced after every word, (personal preference) I will re-type it at the end of this beginning, entirely and some statements may be duplicated, that's okay as long as you follow the thought process and the conclusions there are good doctrine information, and good topic information for you to consider. I placed my e-mail address for you to use, tvots777@gmail.com.

There are many more mysteries of the bible for us to explore. I am putting myself out there. I am being a responsible Christian. I stand by what I believe because I believe my salvation depends on it. Consider that I testify that God gave me the wisdom, knowledge and understanding for both books, if not, I would be lying on the God of my salvation which is not a good place to be. You have an opportunity to consider my writings, place them together and come up with your own conclusion. If it is God's interpretation, it will answer questions that most Christians have that never get answered. When God draws you, he will lead and guide you into all truth. 3 John 1:2.

With both books I have written, I only used the written word to direct your spiritual mind to read with understanding using the keys of who, what, when, where, why and how. This should be applied to every bible story, every church tradition, or every practice performed by you to ensure that you are following the scriptures with a spiritual understanding and not your carnal mind.

Judgement will start at the house of God. When he comes, you don't want to be caught up in false doctrines receiving the reward of the wrath of God. There will be no exceptions. Many will find themselves on the wrong side thinking that they are okay and they are lost. In both books, especially the second, I focused on specifics, giving you an opportunity fellowship of the spirit, to use that mind to find God. You can trust him to lead and guide you into all truth. TVOTS 2.0 is the true Christian's guide to spiritually understanding the KJV bible John 6:63.

Enjoy your study. Ephesians 6:10-17. 1 Corinthians 11:26-32. Verse :26, 'till he come. If Jesus is in or invited into every service, the original genuine article, God himself is with you then what is the need to symbolize the communion with an inferior carnal object? Christians are looking for someone to guide them through the scriptures spiritually to prevent themselves and loved ones from going to hell like the rich man and Lazarus, also like Phillip and Candace's eunuch. Acts 8:26-39.

I have given you the scriptures, not of my private interpretation, but the mysteries of the word of God in spiritual interpretation. The word that have been with us for many decades. An opportunity to handle the word of truth and the spiritual way to look at what is written. John 6:63. John 6:53-58.

With all the calamities, wars and things happening in the world, with no relief in sight, we have a way of escape to choose God's side and flee from the wrath to come. I pray that something in these books enlightened you about the word and give you a hunger and thirst for a better understanding. Psalms 34:8. Amen.

Let's get started. The Voice of The Sword book left off with the scripture in Luke 24:13-53. Jesus on the road to Emmaus. Let us examine these passages, on the road, Jesus found several of the Apostles coming from the sepulcher. They thought Jesus to be from another town, far enough that he would not have known all the things that had just taken place. Reading the scriptures, we know that Jesus was the one that the scriptures are talking about, and they remembered his words. These are the same men that followed Jesus from the beginning of his ministry 3 and a half years ago.

Study the scriptures, don't just read them. You may read over quickly some important facts that you need to consider which may aid in your understanding of what and where they are directing you. The main point of the message, sometimes the main point may not be written, they are just implied. God or Moses is leaving it up to you to search beyond what is written and to think using your spiritual mind and not your carnal mind. What's not written is just as important as what is, it is all in you on how you look at it.

Are you receiving the spiritual understanding that God or the writer intended you to have? Are you following the facts written in the bible? Or are you trying to understand spiritual mysteries with the carnal mind? John 6:63. 1 Corinthians 2:9-16. 2 Timothy 2:15. Romans 8:7-9.

When reading the word, it will open your spiritual mind directed by the word, written or unwritten, and answers questions you may have had. Some people are afraid to allow the spirit to teach them and want to remain in their comfort level considering their thought process to be correct. God will always lead you deeper into the spirit. You may miss very important information about the situation, question your thought process, carnal mind and conclusions you draw. You will find that you were wrong about your understanding. That was the easy part, here comes the hard part, what to do with the knowledge you have obtained. Will you admit to yourself and others that you missed the mark? Are you going to humble yourself and ask those who tried to enlighten you to forgive you for being foolish? James 4:17.

Some of the greatest men of God made mistakes in the bible, John the revelator,

Revelations 17:1-18, Revelations 22:8-9. John was in the spirit on the Lord's Day speaking to the angel, and was instructed to seal up the mysteries of the gospel and eat the book. It was sweet in his mouth and bitter in his stomach. Consider the effect it had on John, the bitter part, causing his carnal mind to be subjective, to go thru the flaming sword of the tree of life and to travel in Isaiah's holy way but still missing the explanation of the rider of the beast that he wondered and admired.

John was going to worship at the feet of the angel and was told not to do it. Research should be done on this person that was an angel, in the spirit and one of the defenders of the gospel, good understanding will come about from that study. It will enlighten you about angels, where they come from, their purpose and the statement of us being compassed about by a great cloud of witnesses. God at that time choose not to reveal who he was to them, Jesus expounding the Word about himself. His word was not for the multitudes, it was for them. At times that Jesus spoke to thousands and did not need a microphone, his voice carried over the thousands people not including women and children. He spoke to the heart, a fact not easily understood. The normal person speaking can't carry their voice over a hundred people at the same place because everyone talking at the same time. Hebrews 4:12.

Strive to obtain this knowledge, ask God to direct your path, an attribute of God and his spirit is all knowing, he is just waiting for you to ask. Have you considered John the Baptist, how he prepared the way for Jesus? John filled with the spirit in his mother's womb, had an impact on the people in those days to repent and be baptized. Then along came Jesus with the word. Finally, the understanding of who

Jesus was became clear to them, and continuing to expound the word. Pay attention to what the hearers said, "Didn't our hearts burn?" as Jesus unlocked mysteries about himself.

Christians will quote scriptures without understanding. Letting the opportunity to question God to get the questions that they may have which God may answer. Matthew 18:20.

God is with us, not just to show up, but to comfort us, unlock mysteries, fellowship with him and get to know him in a more perfect way. The breakdown is not with God, it's with us. God is making the statement that he is with us and shall be in you, then what is the need for churches to symbolize the communion every third Sunday?

Counterfeit, playing church, making an exception or a form of worship that is vain in its use. Jesus is the way, and the churches are creating another way like at the tower of babel, when they invented another way to heaven which was their tower. God came down and confounded their language to stop them. John 6:32-51.

If you eat not the flesh of the son of man and drink his blood, you have no life in you. Is the sacrament unleavened bread and wine Jesus' body and blood? 1 Corinthians 11:28-30.

Why entangle yourself with the broad way when you can travel the straight and narrow? Christians are looking for someone to tell them the truth, like the rich man and Lazarus to prevent themselves and others from going to hell. The body and blood of Jesus should be in every service to taste and see that the Lord is good, discerning not the Lord's body. Why is the church feeble, weak and sick? Because the pastors won't furnish Christians with the spiritual understanding of the word. Psalms 34:8. Because you depend on your spiritual leader for guidance and allow yourself to be fooled. They are responsible for their part while you are responsible for yours. 1 Peter 4:17.

When the wrath of God begins at the house of God, you may be entangled with false teachings, vain worship and carnal minded practices embedded in the church system, you will not escape. God will not allow any side doors or back windows for some to enter, and no exceptions will be made for me, you or anyone else. Ephesians 6:9-20. In this book you are familiar with the Christians' war clothes which each part of the armor protects a certain aspect we should use against the Devil. Above all, we have to take the sword of the spirit which is the word of God. Christians who are uneducated in knowing the word of God are at a disadvantage or defeated to believe easily the devil's lies. Genesis 3:1.

Studying this scripture implies several things like breaking down the scripture by using what is written, not written, what it implies and the thought process of the writer. It is okay to use the who, what, when, where, why, and how to come up with that conclusion and it must be consistent throughout the Bible. 2 Timothy 3:16-17. Proverbs 4:7.

Now the serpent was more subtle than any beast of the field which the Lord God had made. He was in a male form. This is the first time he was mentioned and implies that there was prior conversation with God for him to make an interpretation of what he said to the woman and come up with his conclusion. And God did not start the punishment with the results of eating fruit, his words were focused on the curse and the enmity between the children of the serpent and the woman. Romans 8:4-9.

God who is all knowing, is giving the reader a direction to apply spiritual understanding of what took place in the garden, we should follow his direction. The scripture says that he was a beast. Revelations 20:2. Because of his punishment it implies he is an everlasting being. God giving him his punishment started with putting hatred between his seed and the women's seed. The serpent had to have a seed because just like what God said, do we believe God or our carnal mind? What caused Eve to understand that she was naked? A carnal mind with carnal thoughts. Eve was already naked, after talking with the serpent she became ashamed. Before Adam knew his wife in the fourth chapter, Eve was punished with pain in her conception, who was the serpent's seed and who was the woman's seed.

God cursed the beast for he took God's word and made it into a lie. If the serpent had any children, they would have the same attributes as their father. Ecclesiastes 3:16. God created man after his own image, if children were born of God, they would have his attributes. 1 John 3:7-8.

The Lord God's punishment began with the curse, hatred between children and whatever was done was done to Eve which caused her to realize she was naked. She was another man's wife and was called the mother of all living. The Lord God started her punishment with pain in conception. It is difficult for Christians to let go of the fruit, trees and snakes. Try to understand why God is focused this way. The Lord God was born through the pure bloodline, and that's a fact. The mystery is for us to understand how evil entered the world, and to find out how it came about and by who. Ecclesiastes 3:18.

You must believe the scripture; the sons of men are beasts. This scripture is not a proverb, not a parable, it's a statement. In short God cursed Cain, the one that lied to him, and murdered his brother. A mark was placed on him to distinguish him from everyone else. Those are attributes of the devil. Genesis 5:1.

The generations of Adam started with Seth. Although Cain and his people were on the earth, they are not mentioned in Adams bloodline. How does one become a child of the devil? If God does not respect the person, why did he not have none for Cain or his sacrifice? If the sons of God were created on the 6 day after the image of God, where did the murderous spirit and the lying attribute came from? God blessed his creation and told them to be fruitful and multiply while Cain was cursed and marked, with what mark? Cain exhibited attributes of his father, the serpent the beast.

You now have two bloodlines, growing together specifically the sons of God and the sons of men. This conclusion remains consistent throughout the bible until you get to Revelations final battle good vs evil. Revelation 12:9. Don't limit God in your understanding. The understanding of the bible will grow with time, and you will be directed by the spirit and begin to make sense to you. Also, a hunger for more that only God can fill.

We understand that Moses wrote the first 5 books of the bible, his God inspired writings of what took place in the beginning. There is a lot of controversy about what we believe. Your mind in this case is the most powerful weapon like what we convince ourselves to believe or not, and how we accept what we learned and the process. Our minds desire clarification and assurance of what we believe. We connect with our spirit in seeking its maker. God expands on this part of man, and gives him a thirst for him and a hunger for the truth to protect his mind as if his life depended on it.

Do not be so quick to accept everything as gospel. It could be your carnal mind leading you astray. Ask God to open up your understanding, and to direct it on the path that he want you to go. Mark 9:24. A part of the human makeup is spiritual; it can only be feed with spiritual food or things pertaining to the spirit. In some cases, a guide is needed to give out a clear direction, understanding and clarification. It matters how you believe; our spirit will direct us if we keep it aligned with God's spirit, in many cases by expanding our minds or questioning what we read. 1 Corinthians 14:10.

Some bible scholars skip or read over quickly the first chapter in Genesis maybe because of lack of knowledge or understanding, but there is a wealth of food in knowledge of God in this scripture. It is a mystery that can only be understood when God reveals them to you. In the beginning before God said let there be light, there was God and the bible spoke about how the spirit moved on his God's face and upon the surface of the waters. This would results to questions like what does the water represent? How long was God and the water there? What does the water represent? 2 Peter 3:8. Did God mean a thousand-year day or a 24-hour day? Where did the serpent come from? Where or how long was he with God? Are they the people that the serpent used to dwell in his children? Revelation 17:15. God could not use the blessed people that he told to be fruitful, to multiply and replenish the earth, to allow the beast nature to be born through Adam's line. Remember God is all knowing, so why did God start the process with cursing the beast and his seed? If the serpent could have children they would have the serpent's attributes, his spirit and his carnal mind.

The foundation is the word of God. In the year 1517, Martin Luther nailed his 95 articles of protest on the Roman Catholic Church door in Germany and translated the bible from the scrolls which would become as we know it the KJV bible. These were all the things he felt that was wrong with the church and should not be included in the worship of God.

During that time the Roman Catholic Church was the only source of religion, organized body and accepted worship in the world, Catholicism. In his 95 articles, Martin Luther believed that hearing from God will allow believers to change their mind and give them an alternative way of worship. Today the pope, the leader of the Catholic Church, dropped the name of Roman from how they are referred to detract others from realizing that the church had a major part in killing Christ.

Saul, a student of Catholicism, believing their way to be correct, from Damascus' letters that if he found any in that way, Jesus' way that he could destroy them. Acts 9:1-2. At that time the church was split into two, the Catholic and the Protestant religion. With this split in religious beliefs, they brought along with the split their customs, traditions, ways of worship and accepted church practices. Although God moving by his spirit, was involved in this process, did not mean that everything with the church system was acceptable and the church end result was accomplished. Although God inspired churches, they would believe that the moving of God's spirit in their services would somehow meant that everything they did was accepted by God.

Religion is man's search for God. If God is not satisfied, his spirit will begin to move on men, and they will begin to read the scriptures for themselves and will get a clearer understanding of God. God would give it to them, leading them closer and closer to himself.

From the Protestant movement, other church organizations began to be formed. These organizations would study, hear from God, and believe that they have reached all of God's wisdom and would not go any further. A good example of this process is Peter when he moved by fear. Jesus was trying to show them something and he proposed building tabernacles, equivalent to churches in our time. Matthew 17:5.

God would begin to move again and required still a closer walk with him. So, the Lutheran church, a branch of the Protestant movement was created, others began to follow, they would here from God and limit God to their religion, their way of worship customs and their traditions. With this movement, the polluted way of worship followed, members believing that they had a monopoly on God and became embedded in the church culture. Other religions branched off this movement, Methodist, Episcopal, AME, COGIC, 1st, 2nd, 3rd greater Baptist movement, Pentecost, Holiness all the way down to the Apostolic church. All of them testifying that they have a knowledge of God, and believe that their way of worship is the only way to God. 1 Corinthians 14:10.

Though sincere, in some cases they could be sincerely wrong. Studying the scriptures of Moses' account of the children of Israel, you will find that God had a plan and that they were not just wandering about aimlessly in the desert but that they had instructions, and they were to follow the cloud by day and the pillar of fire by night, the most important fact about this move was to follow God. The children of Israel did not understand God's plan. Their shoes or their clothes were not tattered or worn, none was sick or feeble one among them, and they were provided with food and water. The only instruction for them was to follow God.

My mind recalls a song we used to sing in rounds at the church, "Rejoice for the steps of a righteous man they are ordered are ordered by God, rejoice for the steps of a righteous man they are ordered are ordered by God, in the time of trouble God will uphold you, God will preserve you, God will sustain you in the time of trouble, God will lift you up so rejoice your steps are ordered by God." It is not difficult to see the hand of God move and feel his presence, the hard part is to receive his purpose and his understanding and operate in his time frame. God operates in his time and according to his will. Many instances in the bible where God began to move, Christians, follower's, believers and his people are not willing to wait on God. They begin to come up with a solution, interpretation, or conclusion trying to fulfill or bring to pass what God said. They are operating without understanding. Example is, Sarah giving her servant to Abraham to make him the father of many nations through the servant. God waited years before he opened Sarah's womb to fulfill what he said.

Now listen carefully to what I am saying, an attribute of God is unity, quoting the scripture, where there is unity there is strength. When someone understand this about God, this doesn't make that person correct or right. The enemies of God understand this about God but it did not make them right. Genesis 11:5.

We find that the sons of men, the serpent's children has a purposed in their hearts and minds to build a tower to heaven. To do it their way in their time and we know what happened, God disrupted the process. 2 Chronicles 7:14.

God, often time, refers to his people as sheep. The sheep have no defenses to protect them from wolves, the shepherd or each other. The wolf will travel along with the flock, until he sees a straggler wandering away from the fold and that's his next meal. What was their thought process? Are they impatient, murmuring or complaining of not getting along with the others? God gives us an example of him changing things. John 5:1-18.

Let's examine the scriptures. Jesus the one who implemented the Sabbath day and told all followers to observe the Sabbath, was baptized by a man at the pool that had been there 38 years. Jesus knew that it was against the law or custom to carry or do work on the Sabbath, so he established it. On the Sabbath day, he talked to the man at the pool, we know the story, healed the man and told him to take up his bed and walk. The man obeyed Jesus', and he was shouting and praising God. Here we have the creator of the Sabbath day, who waited until the Sabbath day to heal the man at the pool, who is willing receive the condemnation of the crowd, and who allowed the people to form their opinion, their interpretation and their conclusion of what just transpired.

Jesus is the only one who knows why this opportunity occurred and why, he has his reasons. You can draw the wrong conclusion, accuse Jesus wrongly and operate out of fear or a lack of understanding but remember the entire situation, go to God with your questions and he will let you know that the main point of that situation was obedience. Just like his followers on the road to Emmaus, Jesus had to open their understanding. The opened understanding removes all fear, doubt and confusion of his followers. The progression of the church branching from the Roman Catholic Church to the Apostolic Church can cause confusion, misunderstanding and drawing of the wrong conclusion, so go to God. Hebrews 11:6.

Bible, believer's instructions before leaving earth maybe be viewed as an acronym and a confusing statement. How do we approach God? How do we look upon God and live? A part of our spirit side recognizes his voice. We can trust the spirit directing us toward him. When he speaks, we feel his presence. The very atmosphere around us has a different feeling and some signs of this feeling include goose bumps or your eyes may see a glow and your body acknowledge its creator.

The more you talk about God, the more you will begin to recognize his presence and the moving of his spirit. You can trust the unction by what is being said is what you may have to do or not to do. The more you make yourself available to the spirit, the more you will learn about God. Your spirit will agree with his spirit, it's comfortable, and it gets sweeter and sweeter to the point that you don't want to leave. You'll go in and out and find green pastures. To remain in the spirit would mean departing from this life and meeting Jesus. This is not the end at all, this is just the beginning, and you are now a witness. Any time something good happens, the enemy tries to convince us that it is not real that you have encountered the true and living God. It's personal and a privilege to witness having God's favor, to know you are loved and your name is written in the lambs' book of life special.

You will be craving for a fellowship with the spirit. But the spirit must be feed and it only eats spiritual food which is the word of God. Allowing the spirit to grow, just like the physical body that needs food to maintain itself and grow, your spirit needs food to grow also. The spirit will begin to teach you things and show you things. Get a good KJV study bible and find a spiritual leader to help with your development. If you are unsure where to go, be led by the spirit. Galatians 4:1-2.

We are not alone we have the protection of God's favor and the spirit that is urging us to go onward and upward. Proverbs 4:7. 2 Timothy 3:16-17. Romans 3:4. 1 Timothy 4:1-2.

If you'll notice the beginning of the previous sections, there was a sub text for you to study. There is a big difference in the verb to read and to study. Reading the word is okay, but to study the scriptures is extremely necessary to equip the Christian a foundation of faith and truth. By reading the scriptures, you will undoubtedly miss the main point or interpretation, conclusion and understanding. Studying the scriptures, you will receive the main point of what the writer wants to make, and it will be based on fact, not on your opinion, carnal mind and public opinion.

During Jesus entire life, from the age of 13, he would often be in the temple going over the scriptures. Every time Jesus do his sermons and speaking to the masses, he would take his disciples aside and give them his interpretation and his conclusion of the meaning of what he just spoke about, the meat of the word. You should be a follower of his example, a Christian.

In this section, I have 4 scripture references based on its importance. The devil from the beginning used this method to deceive the woman to make God's word, change the truth into a lie by changing what God said by one word and convincing her that his interpretation was accurate. Also, the devil came to Jesus, the Word himself, to twist him up in the scriptures and to try to get Jesus to eat stones, jump off the mountain, and bow down and worship the dragon. 2 Corinthians 2:11.

We went over the progression of the church. The translations of the bibles and how the devil uses the lack of understanding to trick Christians to believe a lie. With all the bible translations, all the denominations' purpose in their heart and mind to use the scriptures as their foundation, believe that they stand on the word. If the thought principle is not found in the bible, leave it alone. You are wandering into the devil's territory. The Devil is running around in the church, changing God's truth into a lie. If it is not scripture, don't accept it. There should be no middle ground because you will be excepting false doctrines that are making accusations and testimonies about God that are according to man's opinion.

Nowhere in the bible of the 66 books is raptured. If it is not in the scriptures, don't acccept it or make exemption to practice it. Google rapture is nowhere in the bible. Nowhere at any time did God remove any person out of danger before destruction. If it is not in the bible, it's a devil doctrine, no middle ground. Christians who believe on this principle and expecting to be pulled out of tribulation is making a fool of you. Ephesians 6:11-18. Psalms 24:7-1 0. Revelations 17-22.

Armageddon is the final battle, good vs evil. If the devil can get you not to endure or not to prepare to fight till the end, you have already lost. Christians adopt this method, the rapture as gospel, and the truth when it is not because it is hard for them not to follow public opinion when pressured by the masses or the majority. The narrow way is available to you if you'll only study.

Foundation: Consider the importance of a good foundation of the word of God. The interpretation and meaning of what we study. As Christians, we draw conclusions, make judgements about God and about people, follow customs and traditions in our way of worship. We make decisions of what we accept as gospel or what we feel is the path God wants us to go. Not to force feed you at this point, it is very important. Knowledge is increasing in the physical part, so why not in the spiritual? 2 Timothy 3:16. Matthew 13:11. 2 Timothy 2:15. 1 Timothy 4:1. Romans 1:16-20.

Myself as a spiritual leader, I am responsible for speaking the truth. I testify that God himself is giving me wisdom and understanding. What I accept as gospel, I'll have to give account in the day of judgement and my salvation depends on it. Christians quote the scripture, where two or three are gathered in my name there I am in the midst. I'm speaking as the oracle of God; I will be in serious trouble lying on God. There is a record. You, on the other hand are responsible for what you hear, accepting it as coming from God is your choice and there is no excuse. Romans 1:16-32. Institute in your heart and mind to only to accept the truth, the gospel. 1 4:1-5. 2 Thessalonians 2:1-4.

Traditions, customs and accepted practices have creeped into the church and members follow them blindly because the church leadership won't tell the congregation the truth. You can sing a lie and you can make exceptions to your beliefs because it sounds good and all the time the serpent is summoning you to be away from the father. There is no gray area when it comes to God, it is either it will be found in his word or it is not. The confusion is that, so many Christians follow these saying, songs or customs and God is not in it. An example, Christians adopted the custom of wearing crosses which is a substitute for God's spirit, idolatry will make exceptions to why they wear them, and argue with you if you don't agree with them when the word says for us not to do. Exodus 20:4 says any, any means any. You are drawn off by your own interpretation based on what you think and not the fact. The church is full of hearsays, traditions and adopted practices that goes against God's word which are based on one preachers, denomination or faith. Hosea 4:6.

Let us focus on the word foundation for a moment. The result is a completed house, you begin this process with the foundation. You would not build a house without a firm and a sure foundation. This is where it gets confusing, careful study in the spirit stays with me. For you to complete the house, materials must be placed on top of the bottom layer or the foundation. You need a plan of where you want the floor, doors, walls and windows. Then you must put a roof on top of all that. How you build on top of the foundation is important to the house. Stay with me. The floors, walls, doors and windows are not the foundation. They are on top of the foundation as part of the building. You must put materials on top of it which make up the house. You cannot stop the process at the foundation, you must go on to a completed house. The bible is the foundation, the word of God. Earlier I referred to religion as being man's search for God. Once you find God, you have completed the first part of the building, you found him. You no longer depend on someone to direct you to God, you found him. You no longer follow him according to someone's opinion because you can follow him in spirit and truth. The spirit will lead you. Galatians 4:2. Hebrews 6:1-5. Building on the foundation can be difficult but easy if led by the spirit. Proverbs 3:5-6. Ephesians 6:10 -19.

Titus 2:11-15. If you can't remember a lot of what I'm saying, remember this, God with his loving kindness and mercy will always give you a chance and never give up on you, especially if you belong to him. Society with the confusion in the churches, wars on whose doctrine is correct, what translation to believe, God will never give up on you. Believe in him, trust him until this life is over, there is always a chance. Luke 23:43. Luke 16:19-31. Jesus is the only one resurrected from the dead and shown himself still alive after death. You have first graders carrying guns and shooting their teacher, babies carjacking with guns, teenagers taking guns and shooting up the school, the government in turmoil legislating God out of our society. Pro-life, pro-choice having benefits on both sides, consider God's solution, pro God abstinence the best choice. Choosing either side eliminates your options, put God in the equations. The breakdown in our world is the lack of people willing to withstand the stigma of loving, Jesus, going to church, praying for themselves as well as others, teaching young minds the way they should go, not only teach morals but raise the standard in the way they live. We have groups of people standing up trying to make this world a better place through violence, Jesus is the only way to accomplish this. John 18:10.

All these things are happening side by side, Jesus is coming again in his own time and his own way to give this world the best option. Time is winding down and it's later than you think, you have heard that we are in the last days, it's closer now than it was yesterday. We are approaching the final battle, good vs evil, Armageddon, our soon coming king. When given the opportunity to write to you to reveal some of God's mysteries and dispel false doctrines, I could have gone many directions. I believe that it is enough to get you started and well on your way. The conclusions, interpretations and mysteries revealed are not for everyone, just those that are special, spirit lead, filled members of his body, willing to announce that I am one of them, and acknowledge God is alive in them.

God is alive in me, when I stand before him in the day of judgement, to give an account of what I testify to, there is a record of this in heaven and in earth my reward is with him, and he will say it's finished. You are responsible for what you hear and how you walk. Extreme care must be made when you conclude, interpret and understand the scriptures because you can corrupt and provide polluted accusations about God and others. These accusations are lies, disrespect to God and promote your opinion based on your ignorance that you are held accountable for. Scripture is inspired by God; non-scripture is inspired by the devil.

You must be fully persuaded in any instance to side with the Lord and not give heed to fables. Have you heard the mother nature's lie? When you perpetuate that lie, you accept that God is a woman, you repeat it and lend power to it. Others will repeat it and will be accepted as truth. It's easy for Christians to accept it and believe it because it sounds good and could possibly be true. If you accept this false doctrine, what are you saying about God? Is God a woman? In the day of judgement, you will explain to him the conclusion you drew from it. God will say depart from me for I never knew you. Just like the children's book Henny Penny, it's easy to get Christians to believe something but what will be the end. Lies and hypocrisy have slipped into the church, in some cases, the door is opened and these lies and hypocrisy are let in. Romans 1:16-32.

The beast and his nature. Ecclesiastes 3:18. Careful study of this scripture will show that it is inspired by God and is not a psalm or parable analogy. It's a statement that the sons of men are beasts. Ask yourself how did they become beasts? Who is their father? How did they come to hate God? Are they cursed? Does God have to respect them? What are the borders of their lands? How are they distinguished from a son of God? Could there be a mark of some kind? What are their attributes? Genesis 3:1.

How did they know to take God as principal and began to build the tower to heaven, and God himself had to come down to confound their language to stop the process. Today it is hard to imagine the attributes of people. How they can kill with no remorse and commit all manner of sins against God and man. Their beast nature is being exposed, like the story of the rich man. Jesus said that the rich man has the law and the prophets to witness to this lost and dying generation, also how they would not believe the one that was raised from the dead. Who to believe and what to believe when the churches itself are in a state of confusion.

Letting in all manner of idolatry, polluted forms of worship, calling it God and inspires bowing down to the criticism of a few that band together who are caught up in symbolisms and forms of worship when God is supposed to be in the midst. Not saying anything or doing anything to correct it is wrong. What is the purpose of the communion when Jesus is in the midst? Jesus said about the communion, "Do this until I come." You can't have it both ways, either he has come in your life, or he isn't.

The rapture is not scriptural and not found nowhere in the bible. Christians believe that during the great tribulation, they are going to be taken up and away from the battle. There is no bible story that supports this, neither the new nor the Old Testament. If you are counting on being taken away, you are not prepared to endure to the end. The mark of the beast was from the beginning until now to separate or distinguish the sons of God from the sons of men. Circumcision at one time was to show the difference between the two. Now it's the indwelling of the spirit and God is letting the wheat and the tares grow together until his appointed time and separation, the battle of all battles.

Is your name written in the lambs' book of life? Colossians 2:21. If it is not inspired by God, it's inspired by the devil for the purpose of turning the truth into a lie to confuse and draw the reader away from the truth and inspire you to climb up another way. His conclusion or interpretation draw the Christian away from the truth. It will even sound scriptural like the serenity prayer, trying to convince you it is God's plan when it is the devil's plan.

Are we going to pray for serenity or salvation? Ephesians 4:14. It looks good, pleasing to the eyes, it is a prayer that God wants us to always pray, a form of godliness and deny the power of God. I am talking about the serenity prayer which is an adopted prayer in the church where you are convinced with your carnal mind that this prayer is the will of God. The devil will have you reason with your mind that it is the right thing to do, and its contents are totally against the will of God. Study the prayer and what you are confessing, see if it lines up with the word and what God says about you. Don't touch it, eat less, and you will surely die. The great deceiver is at his job drawing weak followers away from sound doctrine appealing to your carnal mind your flesh, your free will and human nature. You cannot survive on this, and you cannot intellectually serve God. He must be worshiped in spirit and in truth.

Google is a very good tool that you can use to research the bible quickly, but when it comes to believing in God or Google that's an easy choice. Look up the customs and accepted practices. Do it line up with the word? Are you looking at it spiritually? Or are you trying to understand it with your mind? What does it say? Will it bring us closer to God or keep us away? Do not touch, handle or taste the unclean thing. If google could not find any bible-based scripture to verify it's truth, conclusion, interpretation or practice, it should not be accepted into our worship services. We should not accept it as such is in vain. Sayings, practices and forms of worship creep into the sanctuary sitting on the front seat of the church.

Counterfeit, symbolically serving God should never be adopted. Disputes about baptisms, we see that when John performed his baptisms and Jesus performed his, they looked for a river to baptize, not go looking for a cup to sprinkle the forehead of the candidate. The great commission commands us to baptize in the name of the Father, and of the Son, and of the Holy Spirit. Not understanding that the father has a name, father is a title, the son has a name, son is a title, and the Holy Ghost is sent in Jesus's name is wrong. When you say those three titles, there is a name attached to all three which is Jesus. Jesus said, I come in my father's name, the son has a name, and the Holy Ghost is sent in Jesus's name. Preachers in denominations and church organizations recite baptisms in the titles not correcting the practice and don't rightly divide the word of truth. When the rich man with the five brothers talked to Jesus, Jesus told him and the brothers to have the laws of Moses and the prophets to instruct them but they won't believe the one raised from the dead, himself. Adding to the confusion of who is right. Romans 3:4.

Hebrews 12:1-2. Moses being led into the mountain by God, was spoken to through the burning bush and in God's presence revealed his plan for him and his people. You can imagine Mosses' agenda was to see God's face, to have that special relationship with him, and to communicate with each other to remove all doubt where his information was coming from. Moses was in the mountain on several occasions over forty days, had the closest relationship with God than any other. Being in his presence, he hid his face from God out of respect and acknowledging his great power and authority.

Christians become satisfied with their experiences, knowledge and understanding of God. People that can swim will only go as far as their ability will take them or confidence in the water. There are those that approach the water, dip the tip of their toe in the water and are satisfied, and accomplishing that satisfaction when it comes to the water level. There are some that will brave the coldness of the water at the ankle-deep experience. You have swimmers that will become braver and walk around the water up to their knees and will go no further. Now you have the thigh deep swimmers that will splash thigh high in the water, although they can swim, they will go no further, possibly thinking that a shark might get them. Cannot see the bottom, supposing a jellyfish might get them, don't like the eerie feeling of the sea weeds brushing up against them. Now you have the waist high swimmer, have a little confidence in their ability but will go to that level and no further. Chest high swimmers may leave the bottom and swim parallel to the beach from time to time, confident in their ability but ever watchful of under tows, rip tides and such that might carry them away. Then you have the bold swimmer that will launch out into the deep, where few will follow because they don't have the confidence in their ability, experiencing the waves and different coolness levels in the water. Each swimmer looking at each other in some cases, admiring others and finding fault moved by fear hoping to reach that level of confidence in themselves.

When it came to Moses, he desired to see God's face. Exodus 33:20. Moses, the only one that saw the glory of God, not all of him at first, but the latter end. This experience caused Moses to wear a veil on his face, so the people did not look upon him and die from the glory shown on his face. Moses was given a small sample of God, giving him a small sample of the depth of him.

We limit God according to our understanding, and making assessments, accusations and judgements against him. When looking up to the point of not being able to see ourselves, someone that is spiritual must guide us to the place of us overriding our opinion and carnal mind. Genesis 1:27.

The verse and scripture speaks about man and woman then God blessed them. It is easy for someone that is spiritual minded to explain this. John 4:24. There is no confusion and contradiction, and should not make the accusation that God's word is fallible or mistaken in it. You are assuming that you lack in understanding and judgements that God don't know what he is doing or there are mistakes in the bible. God is God all by himself. Here we go again, confusion and contradiction Genesis told us, consistent throughout the bible when God appeared, he came with two angels Michael and Gabriel. Consider this, if God was alone in the beginning, he did not need to help with his creation, angels are spiritual beings, if they sin and fall because they do something wrong, their punishment would have to be forever, just like man that was blessed with spiritual being and made after his image.

Consistency throughout the bible, follow Jesus ministry from the age of thirteen as he was found in the temple expounding the word that Jesus spoke to thousands at a time. Isaiah 28:8-10.

Angel's punishment is forever, man's punishment is forever, and the serpent's punishment is forever. It is not known for the most part about God in the beginning, there are mysteries about him that few can comprehend, God operates according to his time. Consider this, is the day a twenty-four-hour day? A thousand-year day? Don't limit God and don't accuse him of things you don't understand, you will have to be accountable from everlasting to everlasting.

Remember God was before Genesis 1:1, how long, we don't know unless he reveals it to us. Where did the serpent enter the scene? How long was he in existence before he showed up in the third chapter? The scripture implies he communicated with God. Is this where he talked to one third of the angels into following him? The thought in his mind was that he would exalt his throne above the throne of God. Is this where the people of the serpent come from? The water was in existence before let there be light was said. What does this water mean or represent? There is a whole wide mystery about God revealed in these scriptures, waiting for someone to unlock. Revelations 17:15. Matthew 25:41. Genesis 2:5.

All of mankind was created spiritual beings according to the series of events, then God formed a man and called him Adam. When he was formed, he had no woman to tend the garden, this must be explained when God created male and female then blessed them. This would imply that God would have to know which spirit that he put in which body, whether blessed or cursed God would know. Now on the other side, Cain's wife needs to be explained. Adam and Eve had other children, female children. Physically she was his sister, but what about spiritually? Where did God get her spirit from? Do not accuse God of not knowing his creation or placing his blessed children in the devil's body. You must study, rightly divide and be consistent. Genesis 11:31.

Sarah was Abraham's sister-in-law, so the statement that Sarah was his sister was correct and not a lie. What would that say about God? He promotes lies, he associates with liars and he use the devil's principle to financially promote Abraham. The servants of Abraham were under strict orders to choose a near kin's woman as a wife for Isaac. So why would his wife be any different? Study the bloodline of Sarah and Rebecca carefully. When loosing at flesh side, they can both say that Abraham and Isaac were their brothers which is a true statement, don't accuse God of being a liar, it's not in his nature. Proverbs 4:7. Revelation 22:8-9.

I have given you the scriptures and broken it down in a way to give your spiritual mind a focus, a direction for your thinking. Romans

3:4. I am not trying to force to feed you the gospel, you can believe what you want and see how far that belief will take you. Consider your thought process. Are you spiritually discerning the scriptures or venturing into the serpent's territory using your carnal mind?

www.ingramcontent.com/pod-product-compliance
Lightning Source LLC
LaVergne TN
LVHW010556070526
838199LV00063BA/4990